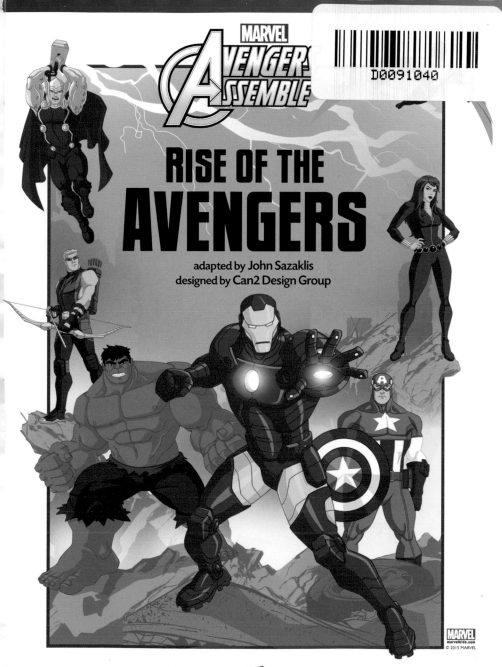

MARVEL
AVENGERS ASSEMBLE

RISE OF THE
AVENGERS

adapted by John Sazaklis
designed by Can2 Design Group

studio fun BOOKS

White Plains, New York • Montréal, Québec • Bath, United Kingdom

Located in the heart of New York City is the gleaming penthouse of billionaire industrialist Tony Stark. Tony is well known all around the world for his vast wealth, movie-star good looks, and his unparalleled intelligence. Among these terrific traits lies another very important aspect of Tony Stark's identity—that of his armored, super powered alter ego—IRON MAN!

Iron Man is Tony's greatest invention. It is a high-tech exosuit powered by the arc reactor energy source in his chest. When not fighting crime, Tony spends time in his lab creating new state-of-the-art technology.

Tony Stark is a genius inventor. He inherited Stark Industries when he was just 21 years old.

2

Iron Man is a member of an elite team that consists of some of the Earth's Mightiest Heroes. Tony's gleaming structure of glass and steel is their base of operations. When brought together, these powerful people are known as the AVENGERS!

Right now he is closely monitoring his teammates. It has been a while since the world needed their combined forces.

The arc reactor is an electro-magnetic device that keeps a piece of shrapnel out of Tony's heart. It also powers his Iron Man armor.

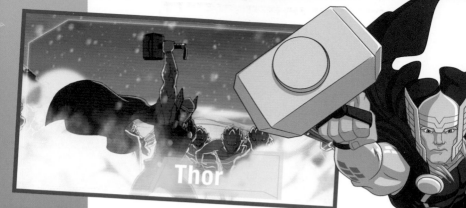

Thor

Hulk

Thor's full name is Thor Odinson. He was born on Asgard and is also known as the God of Thunder.

First, Tony checks on Thor. The mighty Asgardian warrior is in another realm, fighting the Ice Giants. With his mighty hammer, Mjolnir, Thor can command the elements. He calls forth lightning bolts to aid his hand in battle.

Second, Tony checks on Hulk. The Green Goliath is facing off against a giant monster and doing what he does best—SMASHING!

The Hulk's alias is Dr. Bruce Banner. He is a scientist.

Next, the bored billionaire spies on Hawkeye. The snarky archer flips upside-down and delivers a message back at Tony by using the inventor's handsome face for target practice. Tony sighs, dejected.

> LOOKS LIKE THOR'S BRINGING THE THUNDER.

> IT ALSO LOOKS LIKE NO ONE NEEDS MY HELP.

Hawkeye's real name is Clint Barton. He is a skilled marksman with a sarcastic sense of humor.

Suddenly, an alarm blares in the lab. *BREEP BREEP BREEP.* Red lights flash on and off.

Tony nearly spills his coffee from the excitement. It appears his prayers for action have been answered! The billionaire inventor clacks away at the keyboard and pulls up the screen showing the disturbance. He is surprised to see his friend Captain America!

The Super Soldier has his hands full. He is located at the Statue of Liberty, engaged in a brutal battle with a horde of henchmen.

FINALLY! SOME GOOD NEWS!

CAPTAIN AMERICA

Tony uses his satellites to zoom in on Captain America's adversaries and comes across a frighteningly familiar face—Red Skull! Long thought to be dead, Tony confirms that this villain is very much alive.

AND NOW, THE BAD NEWS.

RED SKULL

World War II lasted from 1939 to 1945.

Red Skull is the leader of the terrorist organization known as Hydra. Injected with a serum like the Super-Soldier formula given to Captain America, Red Skull has both enhanced speed and strength. His return means nothing but trouble.

Hydra was founded in the 1940s under Red Skull's direction. It is S.H.I.E.L.D.'s most persistent enemy.

8

SKULL BUSTING MAKES ME HUNGRY!

In Greek mythology, a Hydra is a serpent-monster with multiple heads. When one head is cut off, two more grow in its place!

Time is of the essence. Tony commands J.A.R.V.I.S. to prepare his mechanical armor. In mere moments, Tony Stark suits up to become the armored avenger, Iron Man! Then he rockets out of the tower headed toward Liberty Island. *WHOOSH!*

J.A.R.V.I.S. stands for Just a Rather Very Intelligent System. He is artificial intelligence created by Tony to help him on his missions.

The Statue
of Liberty
opened on
October 28,
1886.

Meanwhile, at the Statue of Liberty, the Sentinel of Liberty is facing off against a horde of Hydra henchmen. They descend upon the star-spangled soldier from every direction.

Captain America uses his expert combat skills, along with his enhanced speed and strength, to quickly incapacitate them with a flurry of punches and kicks. Soon, more reserves appear to apprehend the hero.

It was
designed by
the artist
Frédéric
Auguste
Bartholdi.

Captain America hurls his Vibranium shield with amazing accuracy. It zigs and zags with precision, knocking down each foe in seconds. *CLANG!*

Once all the goons are dispatched, Cap focuses his full attention on his arch nemesis, the Red Skull.

UP TO YOUR OLD TRICKS, SKULL? PREPARE TO LOSE...AGAIN!

HA! I HAVE NEW TRICKS THAT WILL BLOW YOU AWAY!

Red Skull unloads a massive pair of plasma cannons and fires them at Captain America. Beams of white-hot energy blast the hero.

Big and green, Lady Liberty wears a size 879 shoe. That's even bigger than Hulk's shoe size!

The robed figure represents Libertas, the Roman goddess of freedom.

ZAP!

Iron Man zooms onto the scene just in time to see the Super Soldier disintegrate right before his eyes!

Red Skull saunters over and picks up Captain America's shield. Then he sneers at Iron Man.

FZZZZZT!

CAP! **NO!**

SO, THE TIN MAN HAS A HEART AFTER ALL!

The Tin Man is a character in L. Frank Baum's classic story *The Wonderful Wizard of Oz*. He goes to the Wizard in search of a heart.

Seething with rage, Iron Man blasts Red Skull with his rocket missiles. The vile villain protects himself with the fallen hero's weapon.

CHOOM! CHOOM!

Without a moment to lose, more Hydra soldiers in jet packs sneak up behind Iron Man. They plan to knock the hero out of the air. If they succeed, the armored avenger will plummet to his doom!

J.A.R.V.I.S. warns Iron Man of the oncoming attack and brings up a visual image of the flying targets on Tony's screen. Without turning around, Iron Man launches missiles from the back panel of his armor that streak across the sky and hit their marks. The threat is annihilated in the blink of an eye.

Captain America's shield is made of a metal called Vibranium.

This alloy has the unique property of absorbing sound.

BOOM!

THOSE GUYS'LL WAKE UP WITH A HEADACHE IN THE MORNING.

Iron Man charges at Red Skull, but the crimson-headed criminal swats him away like an annoying insect.

> YOU ARE JUST A MAN IN A MACHINE. WITHOUT YOUR TECHNOLOGY YOU ARE *NOTHING!*

BAM!

Suddenly, a portal materializes, heralding the appearance of M.O.D.O.K. The floating super-villain comes to Red Skull's aid and attacks Iron Man with his technopathic powers. M.O.D.O.K. cackles as he crunches Iron Man's exosuit in his mental grip.

> THIS IS GOING TO BE FUN!

WE HAVE WHAT WE CAME FOR. LET US GO.

M.O.D.O.K. releases Iron Man, and the battered hero falls to the ground. Then the two criminal cohorts disappear through another portal. The armored avenger is left alone to mourn the loss of his friend.

His headband enables him to teleport, and his hover-chair is equipped with weaponry.

JARVIS, ACTIVATE THE AVENGERS' PROTOCOL!

15

The cyber-servant contacts Tony's teammates. It sends out an Iron Man hologram to Hawkeye, Thor, Hulk, and even Sam Wilson—S.H.I.E.L.D.'s newest recruit!

SORRY, DIRECTOR FURY, JUST GOT A CALL FROM THE BIG LEAGUES!

BIG LEAGUES?? WHAT IS BIGGER THAN S.H.I.E.L.D.?

00%

Sam Wilson

Sam leaves a training session with director Nick Fury and rushes to transform into THE FALCON!

16

The super heroes meet at the Avengers'
Mansion. Once inside, Iron Man leads them
down a long corridor to a hall lined with
statues of fallen heroes. The most recent
addition is their courageous comrade,
Captain America. Iron Man tells them about
the battle against Red Skull and M.O.D.O.K.
The other teammates are crestfallen.

Nick Fury
takes an
Infinity
Formula
yearly to
increase his
lifespan.

His first
appearance
was in the
comic book
Sgt. Fury
and His
Howling
Commandos
#1 (May
1963).

I CAN'T DO
THIS ALONE. WE
HAVE A FRIEND
TO AVENGE!

WE ARE AVENGERS.
THE WORLD NEEDS US!

HULK SMASH
SOME MORE!

Meanwhile, at Hydra's secret Arctic headquarters, the nefarious duo discusses their evil scheme to take down the Avengers. All of a sudden, an alarm alerts them to an unidentified flying object in their perimeter. It is the Avengers' sleek high-tech aircraft, the Quinjet!

The Arctic is a polar region located at the northernmost part of the Earth.

IT WOULD APPEAR THAT THOSE BLASTED HEROES ARE ON THEIR WAY.

THEN WE SHALL GIVE THEM A WARM WELCOME.

On the jet, Iron Man is at the controls guiding the team toward its target. Hawkeye pulls out a small packet and flings it with expert accuracy right into the Hulk's mouth.

THEY'RE CALLED MINTS. TRY A DOZEN!

MINTS

HAWKEYE!

WHAT? IF WE WANT TO FIGHT THE BAD GUYS, WE GOTTA CUT THROUGH HIS GAMMA BREATH TO SEE THEM!

Hulk grabs the annoying archer and holds him out of the Quinjet's door. Frigid wind comes whirling into the cabin. Iron Man tries to maintain control of the vessel while chastising his foolhardy teammates.

Hawkeye squirms and yells at Hulk to pull him back inside. Thor lets out a hearty laugh at the funny sight.

Suddenly, something catches Hawkeye's attention. Even hanging upside down, the marksman manages to see a cannon hidden in an ice floe and warns the others. Hulk pulls Hawkeye safely inside in the nick of time as the cannon launches a missile at the Quinjet! *CHOOM!*

The Avengers' first appearance was in *Avengers* #1 (September 1963). It was written by Stan Lee, penciled by Jack Kirby, and inked by Dick Ayers.

SEE ANYTHING NOW?

The Quinjet is a high-tech mode of transportation. It is a vertical take-off and landing aircraft with turbojet engines that can reach Mach 2.1.

Thor flies out into the snow-filled air and confronts the missile. He pounds it with his hammer, and it detonates away from the Quinjet.

BOOM!

Another missile makes its way toward the aircraft, but Hawkeye has it in his sights. Reaching into his quiver, the hero loads his bow with an exploding arrow and lets it loose. The second missile is safely detonated, too.

BOOM!

BOOM!

BOOM!
BOOM!
BOOM!

Four more missiles rocket toward the
Quinjet. Iron Man deftly maneuvers out of
their path. He aims the jet's rocket launchers
at the missiles and dispatches them with ease.

Suddenly, a more powerful force attacks the Quinjet. The flying vehicle shudders through a terrible bout of turbulence. Iron Man struggles at the controls as the other heroes brace themselves for what might be a very sudden impact with the ground below.

Then a figure appears on the screen, intercepting Iron Man's transmission. When the figure comes into focus, the Avengers see the gnarled, ugly face of a familiar foe. It is M.O.D.O.K. and he has snared the aircraft in his telekinetic grip!

UH, OH. WE'RE GOING TO NEED SOMEONE TO AVENGE US!

M.O.D.O.K. rends the Quinjet apart, causing it to explode in midair. The heroes eject and land roughly on a nearby iceberg. Before they can recover, Hydra henchmen surround them on all fronts.

KA-BOOM!

SO WHAT'S THE PLAN?

HIT EVERYTHING. *HARD!*

I LIKE THAT PLAN!

Iron Man's first appearance was in *Tales of Suspense* #39 (March 1963)

Hawkeye's first appearance was in *Tales of Suspense* #57 (September 1964).

Iron Man leads the attack with an aerial assault. He launches rocket missiles at the oncoming horde, blasting them off their feet.

Hawkeye backflips and shoots his arrows down the barrels of the soldiers' guns, making them backfire.

Thor sends his hammer on a mission. It smashes through every cannon in the vicinity and returns to its owner's grip in a matter of seconds.

CHOOM!

BANG!

BLAM!

Thor's first appearance was in *Journey Into Mystery* #83 (August 1962).

Iron Man suddenly gets snared by M.O.D.O.K.

THERE IS NOTHING YOU CAN BUILD THAT I CAN'T MANIPULATE, STARK!

AAAARGH!

Out of nowhere, two flash bombs roll in front of M.O.D.O.K. They detonate and blind the villain. A slender figure walks out of the shadows. It is another Avenger—the Black Widow!

Black Widow's real name is Natasha Romanoff. She is a skilled martial artist and gymnast.

FWOOM!

IT'S ABOUT TIME YOU SHOWED UP.

I THOUGHT I'D BE FASHIONABLY LATE.

A Hydra soldier rushes up behind Black Widow and she disposes of him with one punch.

Black Widow's first appearance was in *Tales of Suspense* #52 (April 1964)

POW!

Red Skull frantically summons M.O.D.O.K. from inside his lair.

M.O.D.O.K. opens a portal and disappears along with the Hydra henchmen. Iron Man scans the area for a signature of Super-Soldier Serum. Since Red Skull has it in his system, he will show up on Iron Man's radar.

The armored avenger zooms ahead as his teammates follow close behind. Suddenly, they are surrounded by more cannon fire. Hulk grabs Black Widow and Hawkeye and crashes through the hangar door.

Thor deflects the shots with his hammer.

M.O.D.O.K.'s first appearance was in *Tales of Suspense* #93 (October 1967)

Iron Man's armor provides superhuman strength and durability.

Flying through a long passageway, Iron Man tracks Red Skull to the center of the base. He uses his repulsors to blast open the entrance. The heavy metal door sails across the room and lands on top of M.O.D.O.K., pinning him to the ground.

KNOCK, KNOCK, M.O.D.O.K.!

It has jet-boot-powered flight.

CRUNCH!

Iron Man surveys the area and finds a shocking surprise—Captain America! The Super Soldier is still alive and hooked up to a glowing machine alongside Red Skull. He had not been vaporized, merely teleported by M.O.D.O.K. into the secret base. Without a second to lose, Iron Man frees his friend.

The armor can fire high-energy repulsor beams from the gauntlets and chest as well as rocket missiles from the shoulders, back, and wrists.

Originally a dull gray, Tony's armor was painted red and gold to reflect his colorful personality.

AM I GLAD TO SEE YOU, BUDDY!

The "body swap" plot was introduced in the 1882 novel *Vice Versa* by Thomas Antsey Guthrie, in which a father and son exchange bodies.

Vice versa is a latin phrase meaning "the other way around."

Captain America is groggy and disoriented. Iron Man helps his friend but notices something different about him. His voice and body language are not the same. Suddenly, Cap's eyes glow red and he bashes Iron Man with his shield.

M.O.D.O.K.'s power transferred Red Skull's consciousness into Captain America–performing a body swap! Now, the first avenger is trapped inside his oldest foe's decaying body while Red Skull is younger and stronger. The villain continues to fight Iron Man with Captain America's body.

Freaky Friday, written by Mary Rodgers in 1972, is a comedic novel in which a mother and daughter switch bodies.

THIS IS GOING TO HURT ME MORE THAN IT DOES YOU!

KA-POW!

Quick as a flash, Red Skull grabs Captain America and punches him across the room.

Both novels have been adapted into films.

CAP, IS THAT *YOU?*

YES, TONY. THANKS FOR AVENGING ME.

WE'VE GOT TO GET YOU OUT OF THERE. YOU LOOK HIDEOUS!

Behind them, the evil Captain America rises to his feet. He cackles maniacally and threatens to destroy the armored avenger. His eyes glow red with fiery menace.

He prepares to attack the heroes when– *WHOOSH*–a blur of red and white streaks through the room, startling the three men. It zooms straight at the evil Captain America and knocks him off his feet with a double-fisted punch.

It is the Falcon! And the young hero has brought along some familiar faces.

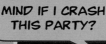

Iron Man is relieved to see his teammates and stands alongside them. Then he utters his battle cry.

Falcon is remarkably gifted in physical sciences, much like his mentor, Tony Stark.

Falcon's first appearance was in *Captain America* #117 (September 1969)

AVENGERS, ASSEMBLE!

At that very moment, a new wave of Hydra soldiers barges into the room. The Avengers leap into action. Hulk stomps his feet into the ground, causing the henchmen to topple backward.

Thor plows through a line of goons with his hammer, scattering them in every direction.

Black Widow and Hawkeye set their sights on the remaining soldiers. The superspy trounces the henchmen by applying her masterful martial arts techniques in a dizzying battle ballet.

The expert marksman dispatches a few foes by deftly delivering his trick arrows and taking the fight back in their favor. Together, Black Widow and Hawkeye make a very daring duo!

By the next couple of issues, the Hulk had been recolored green.

It is not easy being green.

HI-YA!

Iron Man doles out a strategy, giving each hero a designated mission.

HULK AND THOR— YOU KEEP M.O.D.O.K. OFF BALANCE. WIDOW AND HAWKEYE—GET CAP TO THE BRAIN SWITCHEROO THING. FALCON, YOU MAKE THE THING WORK. THE SKULL IS MINE!

35

M.O.D.O.K. frees himself and curses at the heroes.

I WILL HAVE VENGEANCE, STARK. I WAS BUILT TO *DESTROY*!

SHALL WE SMASH?

YES, PLEASE!

Thor and Hulk advance upon M.O.D.O.K. with a special plan in mind.

Hulk pounds his palm against Thor's hammer, conducting a massive bolt of lightning directly at the hovering super-villain. The concussive force sends M.O.D.O.K. and a few henchmen crashing through several walls of the facility.

KRA-KOOM!

Red Skull grabs Captain America and punches him hard on the jaw. The brainwashed hero sails across the room and lands right in the machine. Falcon runs to the control panel. A Hydra henchman tries to stop him, but he does not succeed.

Captain America was not an original team member like Iron Man and Thor. He joined the super hero group in *Avengers* #4 (March 1964)

Once both men are hooked up to the machine, Falcon pulls the switch. Electricity crackles and power surges between them.

Moments later, Captain America and Red Skull are switched back to their rightful bodies.

The heroes enjoy a brief moment of celebration, but the battle is not over. Red Skull has another trick up his sleeve.

MUCH BETTER!

NO ONE MESSES WITH ONE OF OUR OWN AND GETS AWAY WITH IT.

AVENGERS FOREVER!

The super-villain creates an impenetrable force field of pulsing energy and traps Iron Man within. None of the other Avengers can breach it.

It was the original Avengers team that discovered Captain America's frozen body and thawed him out!

WHAM!

BAM!

CLANG!

M.O.D.O.K., YOU KNOW WHAT TO DO!

IF I CANNOT HAVE CAPTAIN AMERICA'S BODY, THEN I WILL HAVE IRON MAN'S ARMOR!

Iron is an element found in the Earth's crust.

M.O.D.O.K. breaks apart Tony's suit and transfers it onto Red Skull, turning the villain into the Iron Skull! Then M.O.D.O.K. rips out the arc reactor that powers the armor. The one thing keeping Tony alive is no more!

SHRRRAK!

Its Latin name is *ferrum* and its symbol on the Periodic Table of Elements is Fe.

The villains cackle with glee at the success of their evil plot.

LONG LIVE IRON SKULL!

The force field evaporates and Tony's limp body hits the floor. As the Avengers charge at the two villains, they disappear once again. The heroes now have a more immediate mission—reviving Tony Stark before it's too late!

Without a moment to lose, Hulk smashes their way out of the base. Captain America lays Tony gently on the snow so that Falcon can examine him with his X-ray scanner.

HOW'S HE HOLDING UP?

IF HE WERE A CAR, HE'D BE RUNNING ON FUMES.

I'D LIKE TO BE A NICE SPORTS CAR.

Tony is in bad shape without his arc reactor and needs quick medical attention. Unfortunately, the Quinjet was blasted to bits by M.O.D.O.K.

Luckily, the Black Widow brought her own ride—a flying S.H.I.E.L.D. car. The heroes pile in.

PROMISE NOT TO RIP THE LEATHER.

IT'S CROWDED IN HERE.

GET ME TO THE MANSION, NOW.

WE'LL NEVER GET THERE IN TIME. IT'S IMPOSSIBLE.

IMPOSSIBLE IS WHAT WE DO. THOR, SHORTCUT, PLEASE!

The Asgardian warrior knows what he must do, and leaps out of the flying vehicle. Rapidly spinning Mjolnir, Thor creates a wind tunnel that carves a passage through the night sky. The S.H.I.E.L.D. car swirls into the center of the whirling vortex at a tremendous speed.

Hawkeye's teeth chatter from the vibration and he hangs onto the Hulk while Tony hangs on for dear life. Falcon continues to monitor Tony's health, but the outlook is very grim.

A vortex is a tubular passage of air.

HURRY! HIS VITALS ARE DROPPING FAST!

At the mansion, the team rushes Tony down to his lab. Falcon lays him on a gurney and inserts electric cables where the arc reactor used to be. Soon, several volts of electricity surge through the billionaire, jolting him back to consciousness.

WHOA, WHAT'S WITH THE JUMPSTART?

WELL, YOU DID WANT TO BE A CAR.

GREAT WORK, FALCON.

COULD YOU SAY THAT INTO MY PHONE? I WANT TO MAKE IT MY RINGTONE.

With renewed energy, Tony walks over to his changing chamber. He commands J.A.R.V.I.S. to load him into his most advanced suit yet—the Mark 50! It is more powerful and efficient than any of his previous armors.

Tony Stark inherited the mansion after the death of his parents.

IT'S GOT THAT NEW ARMOR SMELL AND EVERYTHING. NOW LET'S GO SMACK THE RED OFF OF RED SKULL.

It has three floors above ground, three floors below, living quarters for active Avengers members, as well as a hangar for the Quinjet!

45

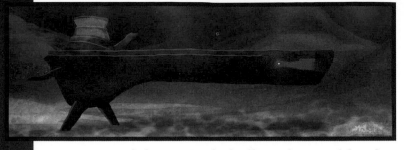

Meanwhile, on Red Skull's submersible, the villains scheme up new ways to annihilate the Avengers.

M.O.D.O.K. agrees and mentions he has sent the Avengers a present, hidden in the S.H.I.E.L.D. car, to help even the odds. It is a small army of micro-bots shrouded in a mist that glides on air currents. This nanotechnology is guided by M.O.D.O.K.'s mind and will give him complete control of anyone who inhales it!

Nano-technology is the manipulation of matter on an atomic scale.

I WILL STRIKE THE AVENGERS WHERE THEY LIVE AND TAKE THEM DOWN!

Back at the mansion, Thor and Hulk enter the training room. They have a quick session in preparation for their fight with Red Skull.

WE'VE HAD SOME GRAND BATTLES, YOU AND I. WHAT DO YOU SAY FOR OLD TIME'S SAKE?

YOU'RE ON!

Thor hurls his hammer at the Hulk, who dodges it with lightning speed. The Green Goliath bounds high and pounds his teammate into the ground. Hulk's victory is short-lived because Thor says one single word.

MJOLNIR!

The magic hammer returns to Thor and slams Hulk through the wall.

CRASH!

While sometimes cocky and arrogant, Hawkeye is known for his playful sense of humor.

Suddenly, the micro-bots fly into the room, and Hulk inhales them. The powerhouse brute is now under M.O.D.O.K.'s control.

His eyes turn red. In a blinding rage, Hulk pummels Thor into the hall of heroes, startling Hawkeye and Black Widow.

Hulk's friends think he has anger-management issues.

GUYS, STOP FIGHTING! HULK IS STRONGEST. THOR IS PRETTIEST. WE GET IT!

THAT'S NOT IT. SOMETHING'S WRONG.

Thor's bulky muscular form slides across the floor of the great hall, leaving a trail of wreckage. Mjolnir lands with a heavy thud next to its owner.

Soon after Thor pulls himself up off the ground, the wicked widgets make their way into his respiratory system. The Asgardian is now under the same malicious mind control and he is MAD!

In Norse mythology, Thor is the son of Odin, the All-Father and ruler of Asgard.

YOU DARE TOUCH THE SON OF ODIN? I WILL TEAR YOU APART, **MONSTER!**

In order to expand the Avengers' influence, Hawkeye became the founding member of the West Coast Avengers!

Thor hurls his hammer at the Hulk, slamming him square in the chest. The Green Goliath tumbles into a wall, crumbling it instantly. Hulk charges back at Thor, punching him across the room in the opposite direction.

During the raging battle, the two titans topple the statues. The mansion rumbles and quakes as its very foundation begins to crack.

Hulk then focuses his fury on his teammates, Hawkeye and Black Widow.

HULK SMASH THE AVENGERS!

Black Widow and Hawkeye arm themselves to attack their teammates. Hawkeye aims an exploding arrow directly at the Hulk. The Green Goliath grabs it and it blows up in his face.

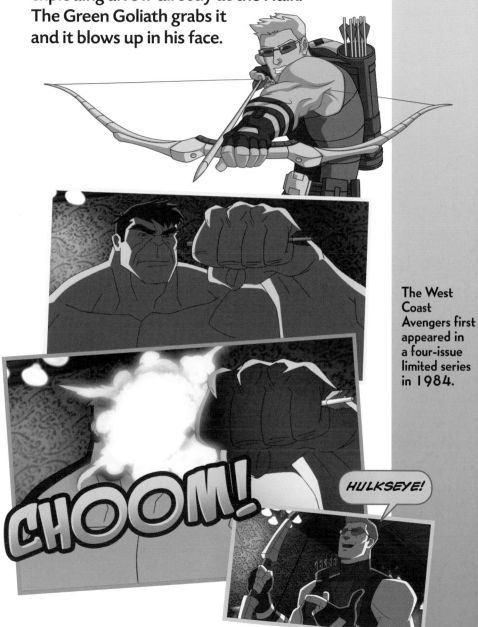

The West Coast Avengers first appeared in a four-issue limited series in 1984.

CHOOM!

HULKSEYE!

Hawkeye turns to Black Widow to see if she liked his joke—but she's not laughing. Her eyes are burning red with rage. She has been infected by the micro-bots!

ZAP! ZAP! ZAP!

With bracelets aimed, the super spy shoots her Widow's Bites at Hawkeye.

The archer somersaults to dodge the blasts. Once he lands, the pesky pests make their way into his lungs, too. Enraged, Hawkeye turns on his teammate and fires away.

FWIP, FWIP, FWIP!

SKEESH!

Widow's Bites' effects can be felt for at least a month and can deliver charges up to 30,000 volts.

Her bracelets can be set to deliver minor shocks that stun or high-voltage currents.

Hawkeye and Black Widow crash through the windows, taking their fight onto the mansion's great lawn. *SKEESH!*

Hulk and Thor continue their own battle indoors until Thor gets thrown through the mansion wall.

Hulk then grabs Thor in a bear hug as the Asgardian pummels him with Mjolnir.

At that very moment, Iron Skull and M.O.D.O.K. teleport into the mansion. They admire their handiwork.

CLANG!

AS PLANNED, MY MICRO-TECH HAS HAD THE DESIRED EFFECT ON THE AVENGERS.

YES, AND WE WILL USE THEM AS OUR WEAPONS!

Thor brandishes his hammer and propels himself from one end of the yard to the other. He charges at the Hulk, who collides into Thor's attack with a double-fisted punch. The sudden impact creates an earth-shattering sonic boom that travels several city blocks, alarming several citizens of Manhattan.

New York City is now in danger of being demolished by the very same heroes who have sworn to protect it!

The Hulk can create a sonic boom simply by clapping his hands together.

Some of the top-secret sections of Avengers Mansion are the arsenal, Hawkeye's test-shooting room, the training room, and the ultra-secure assembly room.

According to Stan Lee, the mansion is based on the Frick Museum located in New York City.

Inside the mansion, the earth-shattering quake catches the attention of the remaining Avengers. Captain America and Falcon rush outside while Iron Man scans the area to find the root of the problem. He sees his friends engaged in mortal combat!

At that moment, Iron Man discovers the threat flying into Captain America's mouth!

MICRO-BOTS! THEY'RE ENTERING THE RESPIRATORY SYSTEM AND SENDING SIGNALS TO THE BRAIN!

Captain America's eyes once again glow red with wicked intentions. He turns his attention to the young hero at his side, itching for a fight. Within seconds, the nasty nano-bots infect Falcon, too!

Now all of the Avengers except Iron Man are under M.O.D.O.K.'s mind-control! The high-tech hero is the only one who can save his friends from beating each other. He needs to come up with a brilliant plan fast!

This building used to be the home of industrialist and art collector Henry Clay Frick.

The Super Soldier and winged avenger had their own fourteen-issue comic book series titled *Captain America and the Falcon* from 2004-2005.

The winged warrior turns to fight his idol, Captain America. The Super Soldier whirls around and clocks Falcon in the head.

Angrily, Falcon extends his holographic wings and attacks Cap with a flurry of flechettes. The bladed darts ping harmlessly off Captain America's Vibranium shield.

Sam Wilson has a pet falcon named Redwing.

STOP HIDING AND FIGHT ME, OLD MAN!

Deep below the Avengers Mansion lies a secret sub-basement with an enormous arc reactor. This giant generator powers all of the Avengers' advanced tech with its limitless energy—and now Iron Skull has discovered it!

The vile villain soon makes his intentions clear. He attaches an explosive device to the reactor and sets it to detonate. This insidious action will result in the demolition of the Avengers Mansion along with its inhabitants!

TO DESTROY THE AVENGERS, YOU MUST FIRST DESTROY WHAT THEY STAND FOR!

Meanwhile, Iron Man races through the large manor searching for the intruders. He sneaks up behind M.O.D.O.K. The armored avenger savors the moment before he unleashes a repulsor beam that blasts the super-villain across the yard.

Mind control is a process affecting your ability to have independent thought.

GET OFF MY LAWN!

With M.O.D.O.K. momentarily disoriented, Iron Man can focus all his energy on helping his teammates. He finally has an idea that will shock them out of their mind-control trance.

Boosting his rocket jet packs at super speed, Iron Man flies into the fray and zaps each one of his teammates with a low-voltage electrical charge that resets their cranial capacity. He feels it will hurt him a lot more than it hurts them, but this act is ultimately for the greater good.

ZAP!

Lightning strikes are most common during the summer. So beware!

ZAP!

ZAP!

The heroes snap out of their trances and look around dazed and confused.

WHAT HAPPENED?

MIND CONTROL, OBVIOUSLY.

The Iron Curtain was the name given to the physical boundary between the Soviet Union and the rest of Europe right after World War II, when the Soviet Union tried to block itself from open contact with the West. This lasted until the end of the Cold War in 1991.

The Incredible Hulk is not pleased with being brainwashed and is looking for revenge.

Hulk grins and pounds his fist into his hand. M.O.D.O.K. is in for a nasty surprise!

J.A.R.V.I.S. alerts Iron Man to another security breach. The hero zooms back into the mansion and catches Iron Skull in his lab.

AREN'T YOU DONE STEALING MY TOYS?

BOOM!

Iron Skull shoots a repulsor beam at Iron Man, but the hero deftly dodges. Then he blasts the villain through the wall.

The Iron Maiden is a medieval torture device with a spike-lined interior tall enough to enclose a human within. It is also the name of an English heavy metal band.

Shock and Awe is a battle strategy based on the use of overwhelming power, dominant battlefield awareness and maneuvers, and shocking displays of force.

Before Iron Skull can recover, he is blindsided by the brunt force of the speeding Vibranium shield.

CLANG!

Hawkeye shoots an electric-charged arrow into the villain's armor, causing it to short-circuit.

ZZZARK!

Black Widow releases smoke pellets that explode at Iron Skull's feet. He is encircled in a thick cloud of gas and momentarily blinded.

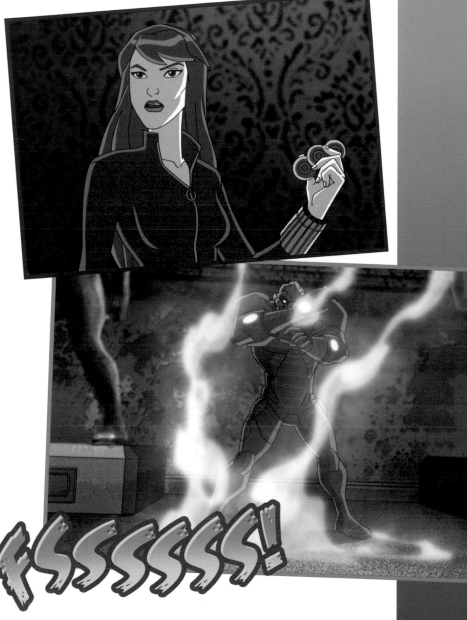

FLSSSSSS!

In 1990, rap artist MC Hammer recorded the hit single "U Can't Touch This" and the lyrics "Stop, Hammer time!" became a pop culture catchphrase.

According to Norse mythology, the hammer of Thor was created by two dwarf brothers named Sindri and Brokkr.

Thor whirls Mjolnir and sends it sailing straight for the Iron Skull. The blow knocks him across the room.

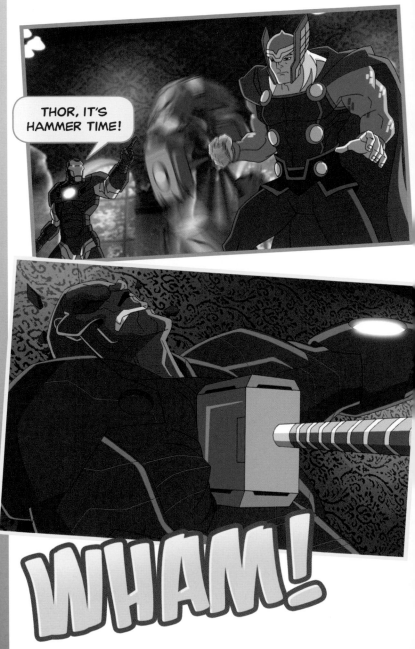

THOR, IT'S HAMMER TIME!

WHAM!

Iron Man scans his old exosuit for weaknesses and tells Falcon where to strike. Falcon fires a series of flechettes at Iron Skull. Each hit staggers the foe and finally brings him to his knees.

BAM!

BAM!

BAM!

The Avengers surround the Iron Skull and wait for his next move.

LOOKS LIKE THIS IS THE END OF IRON SKULL.

Rushing to his
partner's rescue,
M.O.D.O.K. encircles
Red Skull in a glowing
green forcefield. The
villains disappear
through another
magic portal in the
blink of an eye.

YOUR TIME IS
LIMITED, AVENGERS.
SOON YOU'LL ALL
BE BLOWN AWAY!

FZZZZZZT!

WHAT DID
HE MEAN BY
THAT?

In Red Skull's absence, the Avengers are left to ponder his cryptic message. They don't have to think for too long. *BOOM!*

The bomb in the reactor finally goes off. The mansion's foundation is rocked by the blast and crumbles under the explosion. The ground is slowly disintegrating under the heroes' feet. They are now faced with another death-defying challenge and they need to act before it's too late!

The modern-day version of that quote is, "He who fights and runs away will live to fight another day."

The generator rips open. Unable to contain the limitless power supply, it emits an energy beam into the sky.

OK, TEAM. THE REACTOR IS UNCORKED. WE NEED TO COME UP WITH A PLAN OR MANHATTAN WILL BE *DESTROYED!*

SHEESH, NO PRESSURE!

TONY, YOU'RE THE SUPER GENIUS. *THINK!*

Iron Man sends Falcon and Thor into the air to combine their powers and contain the energy beam.

HMM, I'LL NEED SPEED AND ELECTRICITY UP AT THE TOP.

TRY TO KEEP UP, AND GET READY TO BRING THE THUNDER!

The atmosphere protects life on Earth by absorbing ultraviolet solar radiation, warming the surface by retaining heat, and reducing temperature extremes between day and night.

BOOM!

Falcon and Thor's mission is to create a cyclone around the energy beam that will provide a wind tunnel right out of the Earth's atmosphere. That way, it can dissipate harmlessly out in space.

Gamma rays are a form of electro-magnetic radiation emitted by the nucleus or orbital electrons of an atom.

Together, the two flying friends spin faster and faster and faster until they are merely two red blurs to the naked eye.

Iron Man orders Captain America, Black Widow, and Hawkeye out of the vicinity to protect them from the blast.

Gamma is the third letter in the Greek alphabet. It follows alpha and beta.

THOSE OF YOU WITHOUT ARMOR OR PROTECTION PROVIDED BY GAMMA RADIATION, GET OUT NOW!

Then he and the Hulk head down into the sub-basement to tackle the reactor.

The word 'alphabet' is a combination of those two letters!

The angrier the Hulk gets, the stronger he gets.

Sizing up the mass of the machine, Iron Man gauges how much force will be needed to hurl it into the whirlwind created by Thor and Falcon.

HULK, IT'S TIME TO GET ANGRY!

MY FAVORITE TIME OF DAY!

NOW I WANT YOU TO THROW THE REACTOR INTO THE VORTEX.

ROARRRRR!

He is between seven feet and eight feet tall!

With green biceps bulging, Hulk lifts the generator up over his head.

Iron Man takes aim and shoots a full-energy repulsor beam from his exosuit at the machine. The reactor erupts and the explosion gets sucked up into space.

The Hulk also has extremely powerful legs and can leap great distances in a single bound.

CHOOM!

The Big Apple is no longer in big trouble!

The outrageous events at the Avengers Mansion have drawn a curious crowd. New Yorkers are always amazed to see the super-hero team in action. Falcon lands on the lawn and crows with confidence.

The Avengers survey the damage. Unfortunately, their home base has been reduced to rubble. One Avenger in particular laments the loss of the mansion.

I HAD A LOT OF STUFF IN THERE. REALLY EXPENSIVE STUFF!

DON'T WORRY. I HAD ALL YOUR COMIC BOOKS MOVED INTO STORAGE.

OH, OK. WE'RE COOL THEN.

To date, the Avengers have had dozens of members and leaders. Do you have what it takes to join the team?

The Avengers vow that they will train harder and stronger in preparation for any challenge that comes their way—whether it is the return of Red Skull or just rebuilding their mansion.

With their forces combined, the Avengers are unstoppable. They are EARTH'S MIGHTIEST HEROES!